TINTIN'S TRAVEL DIARIES

Publisher's note:

Tintin, the intrepid reporter, first made his appearance January 10, 1929, in a serial newspaper strip with an adventure in the Soviet Union. From there, it was on to the Belgian Congo and then to America. Together with his dog, Snowy; an old seaman, Captain Haddock; an eccentric professor, Cuthbert Calculus; look-alike detectives, Thomson and Thompson; and others, Tintin roamed the world from one adventure to the next.

Tintin's dog, Snowy, a small white fox terrier, converses with Tintin, saves his life many times, and acts as his confidant, despite his weakness for whiskey and a tendency toward greediness. Captain Haddock, in some ways Snowy's counterpart, is a reformed lover of whiskey, with a tendency toward colorful language and a desire to be a gentleman-farmer. Cuthbert Calculus, a hard-of-hearing, sentimental, absent-minded professor, goes from small-time inventor to nuclear physicist. The detectives, Thomson and Thompson, stereotyped characters down to their old-fashioned bowler hats and outdated expressions, are always chasing Tintin. Their attempts at dressing in the costume of the place they are in make them stand out all the more.

The Adventures of Tintin appeared in newspapers and books all over the world. Georges Remi (1907–1983), better known as Hergé, based Tintin's adventures on his own interest in and knowledge of places around the world. The stories were often irreverent, frequently political and satirical, and always exciting and humorous.

Tintin's Travel Diaries is a new series, inspired by Hergé's characters and based on notebooks Tintin may have kept as he traveled. Each book in this series takes the reader to a different country, exploring its geography, and the customs, the culture, and the heritage of the people living there. Hergé's original cartooning is used, juxtaposed with photographs showing the country as it is today, to give a feeling of fun as well as education.

If Hergé's cartoons seem somewhat out of place in today's society, think of the time in which they were drawn. The cartoons reflect the thinking of the day, and set next to modern photographs, we learn something about ourselves and society, as well as about the countries Tintin explores. We can see how attitudes have changed over the course of half a century.

Hergé, himself, would change his stories and drawings periodically to reflect the changes in society and the comments his work would receive. For example, when it was originally written in 1930, Tintin in the Congo, on which Tintin's Travel Diaries: Africa is based, was slanted toward Belgium as the fatherland. When Hergé prepared a color version in 1946, he did away with this slant. Were Hergé alive today, he would probably change many other stereotypes that appear in his work.

From the Congo, Tintin went on to America. This was in 1931. Al Capone was notorious, and the idea of cowboys and Indians, prohibition, the wild west, as well as factories, all held a place of fascination.

Cigars of the Pharaoh (1934) introduced Hergé's fans to the mysteries of India. A trip to China came with The Blue Lotus in 1936, the first story Hergé thoroughly researched. After that, everything was researched, including revisions of previous stories.

Tintin's Travel Diaries are fun to read, fun to look at, and provide educational, enjoyable trips around the world. Perhaps, like Tintin, you, too, will be inspired to seek out new adventures!

The publisher particularly wishes to thank Mrs. Christine Ockrent and television channel Antenne 2 for their kind permission to use the title Travel Diaries.

TINTIN'S TRAVEL DIARIES

A collection conceived and produced by Martine Noblet.

Les films du sable appreciate the contribution to this book of
the following **Connaissance du monde** photographers:

*Olivier Berthelot, Jean-Michel Bertrand,
Maximilien Dauber, Guy Thomas.*

*The authors thank Christiane Erard and
Micheline Baltus for their help.*

First edition for the United States and Canada published
by Barron's Educational Series, Inc., 1994.

All inquiries should be addressed to:
Barron's Educational Series, Inc.
250 Wireless Boulevard
Hauppauge, New York 11788

Library of Congress Catalog Card No.: 94-10456

International Standard Book No. 0-8120-6426-7 (hardcover)
International Standard Book No. 0-8120-1865-6 (paperback)

Library of Congress Cataloging-in-Publication Data

Dauber, Maximilien.
    [Carnets de route de Tintin, la Chine. English]
    Tintin's travel diaries, China / text by Maximilien Dauber and
Martine Noblet ; translation by Maureen Walker.
        p. : ill. ; cm.
    A collection conceived and produced by Martine Noblet.
    Includes bibliographical references and index.
    ISBN 0-8120-6426-7 (cloth).— ISBN 0-8120-1865-6 (paper)
    1. China—Description and travel—Juvenile literature.
    [1. China. 2. Cartoons and comics.] I. Noblet, Martine.
    II. Title
    DS712.D3813   1994
    951—dc20   94-10456
                                                            CIP
                                                            AC

PRINTED IN HONG KONG
4567   9927   987654321

CHINA

Text by Maximilien Dauber and Martine Noblet
Translation by Maureen Walker

BARRON'S

Traveling is a way of strolling through childhood dreams and bringing alive the colorful pathways we imagined in the past.

Taking photographs is a way of expressing our strong curiosity, sharing feelings that some of us have pasted into an imaginary photo album, and which others have pushed to the back of our minds and called memories.

I feel that Tintin belongs in those dreams that are never disappointing because they merely lead up to the actual journey.

MAXIMILIEN DAUBER

Dear Tintin:

And dear friend, too, and I suppose, dear colleague—since our paths have often crossed in the course of our adventures.

Believe it or not, I've just come back from China and I had *The Blue Lotus* in my suitcase. Things have really changed since then. In Shanghai and elsewhere one no longer runs into those strange foreigners who used to make themselves at home everywhere they went—and a good thing, too.

So there I was, sitting on the banks of the Chang River, formerly called the Yangtze Kiang, thumbing through your adventure stories, when a Chinese man politely started a conversation:
    "Well, well," he said, "so you know Tintin, too?"
    The "too" surprised me, and I told him so.

He invited me to his home. There was your collection, translated into Chinese. We spent the evening drinking tea and talking. "I know Tintin and all his friends," said my new Chinese friend, "and Europe, too."

As for me, I wondered more than once if we know their country as well as they know ours.

GUY THOMAS

CONTENTS

The words in **boldface** are found in the glossary on page 70.

HOW MANY PEOPLE LIVE IN CHINA?

One person in every five on earth is Chinese. The most heavily populated country in the world, China has over 1.2 billion inhabitants. A baby is born there every two seconds...

The population of China has always been very large. As long ago as the seventh century, over a million inhabitants lived in **Chang'an**, the imperial capital, whereas Paris and London were not much more than good-sized villages at the time. The population has continued to increase and today China is home to one-fifth of the human race.

In an attempt to stop this tremendous growth, the present Chinese government has implemented a policy of birth control. Since 1980 it has been strongly recommended that there be only one child per family—two at most, if the first-born happens to be a girl. (In China, a son is very important.) There are many rewards for observing this rule, such as receiving a larger place in which to live, and priority enrollment in a child-care center.

In spite of the control imposed on Chinese families, however, it is becoming more and more difficult to house and feed everyone...

Chinese children

WHAT IS A DAY IN BEIJING LIKE?

At six in the morning, the great capital, Beijing, awakes to the calm rhythm of taijiquan—a silent ballet of millions of people...

In the streets, schools, and factories, alone or in groups, the people of Beijing begin their day by practicing taijiquan, (t'ai chi ch'uan) a form of physical exercise in which the movements are very slow and deliberate. The same activity can be seen before breakfast in nearly every city in China. Breakfast, by the way, is a very large, hot meal.

After exercising, the city people go to work. Most Chinese work in state-owned businesses. After eight hours of work, they return home...to their second job! In the last few years, small businesses and private enterprises have reappeared in China. With all this work, not much time is left for leisure activities.

On Sundays the people of Beijing like to be outdoors. Weather permitting, they stroll in the city parks. Otherwise, they watch television or meet for a cup of tea. They like movies, which attract four billion Chinese patrons every year.

The former imperial captial, Beijing, has developed into a metropolis of over ten million inhabitants. It has been the center of power in this huge country since the Ming dynasty.

Top: Performing taijiquan in Beijing
Bottom: Alleys called hu-tong
      Chinese workers

ARE THERE MANY CHINESE FARMERS?

In a country where large rivers compete with mountains for close to eighty percent of the territory, there is little arable land left. Nevertheless, eight million farmers live and work on it...

We cannot begin to study China without taking into account the life of the peasants. Their sheer numbers and their economic importance have always been vital to the emperors of the past as well as the leaders of today. Depending on the region, peasants (farmers) grow rice, wheat, soybeans, tea, or cotton. In areas where there are few rice paddies and fields, horses, camels, or **yaks** are raised.

To increase agricultural output, the Chinese government has decided to no longer take away the entire harvest from the farmers, as it formerly did. For the past ten years, farmers have been able to sell a portion of their products themselves. Thus, open markets began. The profits made by the farmers have greatly improved their standard of living, compared to that of other social classes, such as industrial laborers or government officials. The new wealth of the Chinese peasant depends, of course, on the region where he lives, what he grows, and the number of children in his family.

Over a period of ten to fifteen years, the price of food in China has doubled and even tripled, depending on whether supplies are bought on the open market or the official market, and city dwellers are, of course, not happy about this increase.

Scenes of country life in Guilin in southern China

HOW DID THE CHINESE BUILD THEIR HOUSES IN THE PAST?

To protect their homes against evil spirits, the Chinese used to build "booby-trapped" houses. Anyone trying to get in would have to be pretty clever. Barbarians and demons could just stay where they belonged!

The traditional Chinese house was constructed around a courtyard enclosed by walls that were painted and sometimes decorated. These walls concealed the buildings where the household went about its business. The entry gate was supposed to face south. It was believed that by turning one's back on the **"Barbarians from the North,"** one could keep away evil influences. Behind the gateway was a high wall. Since the people believed that evil spirits moved only in a straight line, all they had to do to get rid of them was to block their way...

The most opulent homes sheltered a garden embellished by a body of water. Little bridges led to a pavilion or a shady garden seat. Today the most beautiful of these typically Chinese places can be visited in Xuzhou, called the Venice of the East.

In modern China there is a shortage of living space in the cities, and families with modest incomes often share the single room where domestic life goes on. The small space available is used to store things "that turn or shine," such as sewing machines, electric fans, bicycles, and television sets...

Top: Garden in Suzhou
Bottom: Traditional entranceway

WHAT IS THE MOST COMMONLY USED VEHICLE IN CHINA?

The bicycle…or, to be exact, millions of bicycles! There are a few cars, too, and lots of buses, but the vehicles that are used most often are those that can be pushed or pulled, or loaded with all sorts of things.

When Beijing (Peking) was still the capital of the empire, the members of the **Mandarin** caste traveled around in conveyances mounted on poles and carried on men's shoulders. They were called palanquins. Richly decorated, these versions of the sedan chair came in various models. For weddings, the bride was taken by palanquin to the family of her husband—a man whom she had not chosen herself. This palanquin was known as the "palanquin of tears."

Today the palanquin no longer exists; to some extent it has been replaced by the bicycle-drawn **rickshaw.** Every town in China offers this mode of urban transport, which is still convenient, fast, and cheap, compared to the over-crowded buses and prohibitively expensive taxis. But the bicycle is the real winner! Used by the majority of Chinese, it stands up to any test it's put to. From family rides to transporting such huge piles of goods that one can't even see the bicycle itself, it's an integral part of Chinese life.

As soon as day breaks, state-owned buses, trucks, and taxis make room on the streets for the army of two-wheelers that invades the broad avenues of Beijing and other Chinese cities.

Left: Area for parking bicycles in Beijing
Right: Foot-powered tricycle,
    or "pedicab"

WHAT IS THE TRANS-SIBERIAN?

Chinese trains have kept the charm of journeys of long ago. Some trains are still steam-powered and offer a choice of three classes: "soft," "hard," and "extra hard"!

Traveling by train in China is an unforgettable experience. The length of the journeys, the varied landscapes, the atmosphere, the unique smells, and the many stops all combine to make this mode of transportation a unique opportunity for in-depth discovery of China. The leisurely pace of the ride, with steam locomotives that never go faster than 35 miles an hour, makes it possible to really appreciate the Gobi Desert or the countless tunnels leading to Yunnan, near Burma. It is remarkable that schedules are so regular on a railway system serving the most remote corners of China.

In the Northwest, alongside the ancient Silk Road, the train still runs on a single track. This causes incredibly complicated shunting by the engineer to allow the train approaching from the opposite direction to pass.

Such lengthy journeys bring to mind the epic story of the **Trans-Siberian**, the 5,000-mile railroad built at the end of the nineteenth century by order of Tsar Alexander III to link Russia to the Pacific Ocean. This line later made it possible to reach Beijing by crossing either Mongolia or **Manchuria**, depending on one's choice of route. It can still be done today.

Left: Steam locomotive in Manchuria
Right: Transmanchurian railroad car

WHY DID THE CHINESE BUILD THE GRAND CANAL?

The Chinese have undertaken some giant enterprises to link together the provinces of their vast territory. In the sixth century they began to build a canal, one of the longest in the world...

The two great rivers of China are the Huang He, called the Yellow River, and the Chang, formerly known as the Yangtze and sometimes erroneously called the Blue River. Both flow from west to east, but in the north of China there was no natural river link. Therefore, in the sixth century, the emperor ordered the digging of the "Imperial Canal," which was to follow a course over 1,000 miles long. This waterway was to allow rice, silk, and many other products to be transported much more quickly than on the crowded roads.

To carry out this gigantic undertaking, a large work force was used. Over the centuries, work on the waterway was interrupted by wars, famines, and floods. Millions of excavators and entire generations of engineers erected dams and locks to control the water level. From one period to another, the ability to navigate the full length of the river depended on the state of repair of the project.

Even today, barges and **sampans**, loaded with coal or bales of silk, pass under the arch bridges. There are always incredible bottlenecks resulting from the comings and goings of all these vessels, punctuated with shouts and the rumbling of engines.

Top: The big canal in Suzhou
Bottom: A bottleneck on the big canal

WHY IS THE YELLOW RIVER CALLED THE "RIVER OF SORROW"?

Powerful and unpredictable, the muddy waters of the Yellow River flow along a course of almost 3,000 miles. In the past, when it flooded, it washed away everything in its path...

The source of the Huang He, the river of North China, is high in the mountains of Tibet. Its characteristic yellow color is due to loess, a rich loam that the river washes away from the land in the upper reaches of its course and later deposits downstream in the plains, thus raising the level of its own bed! For this reason, it has always been necessary to erect levees to contain the water.

Because its flow is so erratic, the Yellow River is still hard to tame, changing direction many times before emptying into the China Sea.

The history of China is in part linked to that of the river, which, according to its moods, used to flood large amounts of land, leaving famine and desolation in its wake. In an effort to tame it, the ancient Chinese used to recite prayers, and offer gifts and even a fiancee! Every year, during a ritual ceremony, a young woman, dressed in a wedding gown, was secured to a bed and thrown into the river, which washed her away. But the Yellow River floods have also performed great services for China. In 1938, when the Japanese invaded, the Chinese deliberately tore down the levees in order to slow the advance of the **Nipponese armies.**

Today the new electricity-producing dams and the diversion channels irrigating the land make the Huang He a valuable ally in the modernization of China.

The overflowing Yellow River
Inset: The Shanghai-Hou Kou railroad tracks

WHAT ARE THE "TEN THOUSAND SMALL TRADES"?

Five thousand years of history and day-to-day living... Chinese tradesmen and street vendors have always continued to develop endless varieties of small businesses. Since nothing is ever wasted in China, these businesses are still present today.

Many small trades, whose secrets are known only to the Chinese, can be found today on the market squares. The feeling of the Chinese for trade may be measured by the unbelievable selection of goods offered at stalls and in little shops. Everything is subject to bargaining—from basic foodstuffs to rusty nails, from medicine to so-called "magic potions."

In the street, **bonesetters** boast about the effectiveness of powdered rhinoceros horn; they also offer serpent scales, **toucan** beaks, and dried rat or lizard entrails. A magician performs his tricks and a secondhand dealer sells popular novels. A birdseller walks among them with full cages hanging from both ends of a bamboo pole. Further on, the ear-cleaner plies his trade and, for the price of a few **fens**, the cricketseller offers the singing insect as a companion.

Musicians play their tunes in markets and public gardens; they often accompany a storyteller whose fame—if he has any talent—will extend far beyond the borders of the province. Theater and opera groups go on tour, stopping in small villages, while astrologers and soothsayers feed the superstitious nature of the Chinese with their predictions.

Top: Cricket seller on the street in Beijing
Bottom left: A photograph of the Forbidden City
Bottom right: A dentist

WHAT IS THE ROLE OF THE ELDERLY IN CHINESE LIFE?

In Chinese civilization, grandparents have always been venerated and respected. The elderly are society's wise people and adults and children alike owe them obedience and support.

Traditionally, the Chinese family, whether rich or poor, was large. Three generations lived together under one roof—children, parents, and grandparents, surrounded by uncles and aunts, cousins, sisters-in-law, etc. From the patriarch, the head of the family, to the most modest servant, everyone had a place, according to a well-established order.

From the beggar to the emperor, the sense of hierarchy also played a role in social life and in relationships with others. This moral system was preached by Confucius over twenty-five hundred years ago. Even today, to some extent, this concept of respect for the elderly influences the Chinese way of life.

And so, especially in the countryside, grandparents are often seen caring for their grandchildren and the entire household, while parents are working in factories or in the fields. Retirement homes certainly have not yet made their appearance in China, and it is considered very inappropriate to abandon elderly relatives.

Old people

HOW IS SILK MADE?

Silk is produced by the secretion of a caterpillar, called, for that very reason, the silkworm. This natural fiber, known to the Chinese for nearly four thousand years, has long been the subject of a jealously guarded secret!

The silkworm is the larva of a moth that has the odd name of *Bombyx mori*. To protect itself while becoming a moth, the caterpillar makes a cocoon by secreting a fiber around which it wraps itself. This fiber—which may be nearly three-quarters of a mile long—is made of a particular substance: silk. It was while observing the life cycle of the *Bombyx mori* that the Chinese came up with the idea of using the silkworms and raising them. Thus, they invented **sericulture.**

From the laying of the eggs to the point at which the thread is ready for weaving, a long series of operations takes place. Fed on mulberry leaves, the caterpillars, arranged on mats in a safe place, reach their maturity in a few weeks and soon wrap themselves in cocoons. Smoke is quickly blown over them to kill them before they destroy the silky covering in the process of becoming moths. The cocoons, carefully sorted, are then scalded to make them flexible and to allow the fibers to be unwound. Braided together (from seven to thirty strands, depending on the desired quantity and thickness), the fibers become silk thread. All that remains to be done is to make the thread round, flexible, and dry. It is now ready for the loom, from which will come the world's finest fabric.

Top: Dipping cocoons into hot water
Bottom: Cleaning skeins of silk

WHAT IS THE SILK ROAD?

From China to the Mediterranean by land and sea, caravans and ships carried the silk, as well as cinnamon and rhubarb, to barter for gold, ivory, and horses...

Trade routes had long linked China and the Mediterranean. Leaving the empire by the north-west, one of the routes passed through Turkestan, Afghanistan, Persia (Iran), Iraq, and Turkey... as far as Byzantium (now Istanbul). For over a thousand years, the Silk Road—truly a link between East and West—was to foster the blending of races, religions, arts, and cultures.

It was by this route that **Buddhism** came into China; by this route, too, the Venetian **Marco Polo** reached China in the course of his famous journey in the thirteenth century. It is said that by this route, around the year 550 A.D., two Byzantine monks managed to smuggle out some *Bombyx mori* larvae concealed in their bamboo canes, and reveal the secret of silk to the rest of the world.

In China those who made up the Mandarin caste—court dignitaries, educated men, and high officials of the empire—wore silk. The delicate nature and quality of the material, the embroidery patterns, and the colors signi-fied the person's rank. Only the emperor wore yellow. The ordinary man usually wore simple cotton garments, similar to the uniforms that **Mao** was to impose on Communist China centuries later.

Top: Muslim in the Xinjiang Mountains
Bottom: Yurt (Mongol tent)

WHAT DO THE CHINESE EAT?

The Chinese are gourmets and eat all sorts of things: monkey, bear, snake, swallows' nests, "hundred-year-old" eggs...and pasta—which they invented.

In China regional cuisine uses local products, of which, because of the size of the country, there are usually a large variety. Northern cuisine (Mandarin) features garlic and scallions; Southern (Cantonese) food has few seasonings and is often stir-fried or steamed; Western (Szechuan or Hunan) cuisine is usually hot and spicy but can also be sweet and fragrant; Eastern food consists of fish and seafood, soy sauce, and sugar.

Filled rolls, noodles, rice with vegetables, and dried melon seeds are some of the dishes usually sold on the street. Meat, fish, vegetables, and fruit are cut into little cubes and cooked. People eat with chopsticks—two very skillfully handled wooden sticks. (It is believed that contact with metal knives or forks might spoil the taste of the food.) Obviously, managing chopsticks is particularly tricky with pasta!

For health reasons, the Chinese attach great importance to the properties of the foods that make up their meals. For instance, in Canton it is not considered advisable to eat dog in the summertime. And pregnant women are advised to eat soup made of fish and beans until they give birth.

Top: Traditional Chinese dishes
Bottom: Chinese family
     enjoying a traditional
     meal in Shanghai

WHY DO THE CHINESE GROW RICE?

On the plains of southern China, every square yard of arable land is a patch of rice paddy. The crop is gathered by hand twice a year, by workers standing in water and often in the rain.

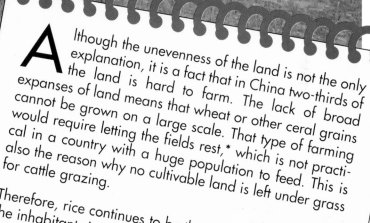

Although the unevenness of the land is not the only explanation, it is a fact that in China two-thirds of the land is hard to farm. The lack of broad expanses of land means that wheat or other ceral grains cannot be grown on a large scale. That type of farming would require letting the fields rest,* which is not practical in a country with a huge population to feed. This is also the reason why no cultivable land is left under grass for cattle grazing.

Therefore, rice continues to be the staple food of most of the inhabitants in China. Grown on small flooded patches of land called rice paddies, it calls for no changes in farming methods from one harvest to the next. A large work force is needed in order to maintain the channels, prepare the seed grain, and replant. Most of the work is done by hand, with occasional help from water buffalo.

The Chinese rarely consume milk products, cheese, or meat because they cannot produce them. Meat is scarce, except for pork—for the pig is an animal that does not need much room and can be fed on household scraps. Other animal meats, even donkey, dog, and rat, are not disdained in Chinese cuisine.

Top: Cultivating rice
Bottom: Terraced rice paddies

*Also called "leaving fallow."

HOW DO THE CHINESE USE CORMORANTS FOR FISHING?

Dark-plumed cormorants live on the seashore and frequent the riverbanks. They are excellent divers...

Although they are found all over the world, cormorants live mainly in cold and temperate regions. In the heart of one of the most beautiful locations in China, famed for the splendor of its rocky peaks, men have trained these birds to fish. The area is Guilin, along the Lijiang River.*

At sundown, flimsy bamboo rafts float with the current. They carry a lighted lantern to attract the fish. A wicker basket is placed in the middle of the raft, and the cormorants sit on the basket with outspread wings. To prevent them from flying away, the fishermen tie the birds' feet to the raft with string.

As soon as the fish approach, the cormorants dive down upon their prey, seize them in their claws, and try, not surprisingly, to eat them. A ring placed around their necks, however, prevents them from swallowing. The fisherman, then, takes the fish out of the cormorant's beak, and rewards the bird with a piece of his catch.

Top: Fishing for cormorant
Bottom: A cormorant

*Because of its beauty, this spot is a favorite place for young Chinese couples to spend their honeymoon.

WHAT IS THE FAVORITE DRINK OF THE CHINESE?

In China the national drink is tea. The Chinese drink it at any time of day and anywhere—but never with meals.

Legend has it that during his stay in China in the year 526, the Indian monk Bodhidharma was one day overcome by sleep—a very inappropriate position for a wise man who was supposed to be meditating! To avoid having it happen again, he tore off his eyelids. They fell to the ground, and on that spot, tea plants began to grow. After boiling the leaves and drinking the brew, the monk felt refreshed. Since then the leaves of the plant, fermented, dried, then infused, are said to prevent sleepiness.

As early as the sixth or seventh century, "tea houses" offered many varieties of the drink. The color, the aroma, and the ingredients vary from region to region, as do the preparation ceremonies. Green, red, or white, flavored with jasmine, bergamot, lotus, rose, or chrysanthemum, China tea is served in "ten thousand" ways. In Tibet it can be prepared with flour and with salt, and in Mongolia with rancid butter and salt!

Even today, many faithful customers still frequent tea-houses, where they enjoy the typically Chinese passion for gambling and gossip.

Top: A teahouse in Aksu
Bottom: A tea vendor
on the street

WHY IS CHINESE WRITING DIFFERENT FROM OURS?

The Roman alphabet is made up of only 26 letters, but the Chinese have to know over 5,000 to 10,000 characters to read a newspaper! Chinese writing requires endless patience!

In order to communicate their thoughts, the Chinese first used drawings. As time passed, the drawings became signs, then pictures or symbols, called **ideograms.** These are the "characters" of Chinese writing. The traces of drawing still faintly discernible behind the purity of lines, the enchanting overall look of the ideograms—there are 30,000 of them—all contribute to making Chinese writing one of the world's most beautiful.

But should we really be calling it "writing"? Isn't it really painting? Or, to be more exact, calligraphy, the art of the brush stroke, in which people express themselves according to their talent and the mastery they have acquired...

Whereas Chinese writing is identical throughout the country, the variety of spoken dialects means that a Cantonese may have trouble understanding a native of Beijing, and so on. Therefore, the television stations, which broadcast their films and programs in Mandarin,* use subtitles to be sure they are understood in every region of the country.

Top: Chinese characters (ideograms)
Bottom left: Same
Bottom right: Bas-relief on temple wall, representing an ideogram that means "man"

*Madarin is the offical language in Beijing.

WHAT ARE THE POWERS OF THE DRAGON?

Marvelous animals populate the universe of Chinese legend. The dragon, the phoenix, the white tiger, the tortoise—all are said to be endowed with beneficent powers.

The avenue of **Ming** tombs, near Beijing, is lined with strange stone animals. For over five hundred years, lions, camels, elephants, and horses have watched over the cemetery where the emperors sleep. But the marble statues along this avenue also represent **unicorns, chimeras,** and other fabulous monsters. Each of them has its own particular gifts.

For instance, the tortoise, with its shell as round as the sky that envelops the earth, represents the universe. It symbolizes great age and longevity. The dragon possesses extraordinary powers of protection. From the emperor to the humblest of his subjects, this animal, found in private homes, on objects, and on clothing that it decorates with a thousand flames, is believed to bring prosperity and happiness. The phoenix—a strange animal with the body of a peacock or a dragon and the head of a pheasant—symbolizes the sun and the heat, the summer season, and the south.

In China, every natural element, such as plants and flowers, is endowed with power or filled with meaning. For example, the orchid is a sign of purity; the chrysanthemum means good health; bamboo signifies wisdom and courage...

Top: Metal dragon at the Beijing Observatory
Bottom: Roof of a monastery in the Shanxi

WHY DO THE CHINESE LIKE TO PAINT MOUNTAINS?

To a Chinese artist, there is nothing more beautiful then the rocky side of a mist-shrouded mountain with a few trees desperately clinging to it...

The Chinese have always been able to express themselves sensitively using art. Through painting, calligraphy, and poetry, they express, on rolls of silk or paper, their love of nature.

Using the same brush for painting and calligraphy—one with an extremely fine point—and mainly black ink made of pine soot and glue, artists, often using only a few strokes, draw their favorite subjects: misty mountains and valleys, waterfalls, windblown pine trees, birds, flowers, or bamboo. Artists also love to paint landscapes, in which opposing but complementary elements, the visible and the invisible, the empty and the full, are depicted. This is the subtle play of opposites, expressed by the Chinese through the ideas of **yin** and **yang.** Thus, studying a painting makes it possible to "mount the thousands of steps that lead to the portals of the Chinese soul."

At one time, color, made from vegetable or mineral pigments, was used only to represent scenes at the imperial court or to tint the frescoes of Buddhist grottoes, which tell of a thousand years of Chinese religious history.

Huang-Xian mountains

IS GOD CHINESE?

In ancient China the emperor, who was called the Son of Heaven, was responsible for maintaining order and harmony in his country. If he governed with wisdom, he continued to have the gratitude of the gods.

It is said that China is the country of the three religions: Confucianism, Taoism, and Buddhism. The first two came into being around the fifth century B.C. Buddhism came to the empire from India, via the famous Silk Road, around the first century A.D.

Strictly speaking, **Confucianism** is not a religion but rather a system of ethics preached by K'ung Fu-Tzu, a philosopher and writer known in the West as Confucius. A code of social behavior, this movement advocates respect for a hierarchical order in which each person has a place and a role—from emperor to commoner, from father to son—and should have good moral character. **Taoism**, inspired by the writings of **Lao-tzu** (or Lao-tze), aims to bring man into harmony with nature through Tao, the road to truth. Buddhism, philosophy of existence, exhorts man to find his salvation within himself. It calls for strict moral standards and belief in life after death. Buddhism was to have a tremendous impact on China, leading to the building of large numbers of pagodas and statues in honor of Buddha throughout the empire.

After more than forty years of communism and prohibition, these religions are tolerated today and are still practiced by the elderly and a few minority groups within the country.

Top and bottom left: Statues of Buddha at the Xuanzongsi monastery
Bottom right: A Buddhist monk

WHY DID THE CHINESE BUILD A GREAT WALL?

To protect themselves from nomadic warriors, the Chinese built a wall—so long that it can be seen from as far away as the moon...

21

China has always had to protect itself against invasions by **nomadic** peoples living on its borders. For this reason, the Chinese built a wall, which, as centuries passed, they strengthened and added to until it was 1,500 miles (2,415 km) long. The wall runs north and west across the empire from the Bo Hai Gulf to the edge of the Gobi Desert.

Originally, it was not one single wall, but a series of separate protective enclosures. These walls were designed to mark the limits of civilization and to keep out the Barbarians from the North. Combined and then restored by successive emperors for over one thousand years, they became the Great Wall. Up to 30 feet (10 meters) tall and 20 feet (7 meters) wide, it was protected by some 25,000 towers spaced about 130 yards (100 meters) apart. Messages were sent from tower to tower by means of signals—flags by day and torches by night—the forerunners of our modern telecommunications methods. This "stone boulevard," in the true sense of the word, also enabled travelers and correspondence to get to the distant provinces in the north and in the east of the empire.

The Great Wall of China

WHO LIVED IN THE FORBIDDEN CITY?

In the middle of Beijing there still stands an impressive architectural complex; Chinese and tourists now come in crowds to explore it. In the past, however, it was impossible to enter it... It was the Forbidden City, the home of the emperor!

Constructed in the fifteenth century, the Forbidden City, a "city within a city" looms as a masterpiece of Imperial China, with its palaces, parks, and gardens spread over 178 acres (72 hectares).* Protected by high walls through which it was forbidden to pass, the emperor and his court lived there.

In the middle of the city is the throne room, where the sovereign received the privileged few allowed to approach him. The adjoining buildings housed his family, and his eunuchs, servants, and guards. Strict protocol controlled the tempo of court life, a life of luxury and splendor, but also a life overshadowed by jealousies, intrigues, and plots.

The emperor's power over his subjects was limitless, but he had no equal except his terrible loneliness. The palace guards jealously screened comings and goings. At sunset the heavy wooden gates insulated the Forbidden City from the rest of the world; even the emperor himself could not have them opened. **P'u-yi,** the last emperor, passed through the gates for the final time upon his abdication, on February 12, 1912. It marked the end of the long history of Imperial China.

Top and bottom left: The Forbidden City in Beijing
Bottom right: The Throne Room in the Forbidden City

*Equal to 144 regulation football fields

23

WHO WAS MAO?

The first emperor, Qin Shi Huangdi, reigned over China 2,200 years ago. Since then, the long history of the "Middle Empire" has been shaken by many invasions and revolutions.

The vast country of China, periodically overcome by devastating floods or famines, experienced many uprisings. These terrible peasant revolts overturned emperors incapable of feeding their people or ruling wisely.

In the middle and the end of the nineteenth century, the empire was shaken by violent insurrections. The **Taiping,** and later the **Boxers,** attempted to overthrow the reigning Manchu, a dynasty of foreign origin that had demanded that all Chinese wear a braid (pigtail). They wanted to make China strong again to face up to the colonialism of the Western nations.

The young **Mao Zedong** believed that communism was the solution that would bring the country out of chaos and poverty. Supported by the peasants, he took power in 1949 after fighting the Japanese and driving out the Chinese nationalists (who fled to Taiwan, where they remain today). Mao wanted to divide up the land and bring equality to the Chinese. From then on, farms and businesses belonged to the state, which took care of everything and made all the decisions. But the popular enthusiasm of the early years died with the sinister **Cultural Revolution** of 1966–1976, during which universities were closed, radicals seized power of local governments, and there was so much violence throughout the country that the army was called in to restore order.

Entrance to the Forbidden City; bust of Mao Zedong

24

DO CHINESE TORTURES STILL EXIST?

The Chinese are an ingenious race... a trait that led them in the past to invent some appalling means of torture! Although these tortures are no longer used today, the fate of prisoners is still less than enviable.

Throughout the world, convicts were at one time subjected to atrocious punishments. The Chinese managed to show great imagination in the punishment of their prisoners.

The "lightest" penalty was beating—4 to 100 blows with a bamboo cane. A man might also be condemned to have his ears cut off or be shut inside a tiny cage. The frame torture consisted of placing a piece of wood weighing over 80 pounds (40 kilos) around the convict's neck. He was not able to sleep or rest, and the slightest fall could break his neck and kill him.

Of course, the Chinese were no worse than the rest of the world, which was crucifying convicts, breaking them upon a wheel, or impaling them. Today, in democratic countries, although this is still not the case in China, every prisoner is entitled to the services of a lawyer. It is obvious that we are better off living in our time, even though we are still confronted too often by depressing scenes of cruelty.

Punishing criminals by using pillories

25

WHERE DOES THE GIANT PANDA LIVE?

With its comical black eyeglasses, the panda lives like a large, lonely old Mandarin in the depths of the humid forests in southwest China. There, in the foothills of the Himalayas, it finds an abundant supply of its favorite food—bamboo.

The giant panda, whose name is of Nepalese origin, is a mammal weighing over 200 pounds (100 kg). Like the bear, it climbs trees. Bamboo leaves and shoots are its favorite food; it crunches over 26 pounds (12 kg) of them every day! The panda will also eat fruit, roots, and eggs. Although it is mainly vegetarian, it does not turn up its nose at an occasional selected insect or small rodent. A solitary animal, the panda seeks a companion only in the mating season. It then builds a cozy nest lined with dead leaves where its young will be born.

At one time the panda's beautiful fur was much sought after and hunters did not hesitate to kill the animal. But today, to protect what has become one of the symbols of China, the government has banned panda hunting. Will that prevent the extinction of this animal whose forest habitat and food are increasingly threatened?

The giant panda has a "little cousin" called the lesser panda, which has a reddish coat and weighs under 10 pounds (4 kg). It lives on the southern slope of the Himalayan range.

Left: A giant panda
Right: A red, or lesser, panda

26

ARE ALL THE CHINESE ACTUALLY CHINESE?

There are about one billion true Chinese, or Han. Their territory covers only about half of China. The other inhabitants, who are not of Chinese origin, are called "minorities."

In China, seven percent of the population is not of Chinese origin. Mongols, Tibetans, Manchurians, and Tatars are ethnic groups that lived on the periphery of the empire before becoming part of it. Even after integrating, their specific characterisics continue to find expression through their languages, their cultures, and their own particular traditions. Described as **minorities,** these ethnic groups are all too often considered by true Chinese to be the descendants of the barbarians who attempted to invade the country long ago.

From the Turkish-Mongol populations in the northwest—such as the Uighurs or Kazakhs, who are for the most part Islamic—to the Miao of Yunnan, in the south, along the Burmese border, an extraordinary ethnic diversity characterizes the population of nearly 60 percent of China.

Some minorities, like the Islamic Hui, are fully integrated into Chinese society. Others, like the Tibetans, are still seeking the return of their independence.

Left: A resident of Hunan
Right: A Han child

27

WHERE DO THE "RIDERS OF THE WIND" COME FROM?

The Mongols, who are nomadic, have always loved the endless steppes (grassy land) that allow them to chase the wind on horseback to the ends of the earth...

For thousands of years the inhabitants of the steppes vied for power in Mongolia. The countryside where the riders of the wind wandered is a huge plateau capped by mountains and characterized by the sometimes icy, sometimes burning loneliness of the Gobi Desert. Beginning in the third century B.C., to protect themselves from invasions, the Chinese erected a series of walls that later formed the Great Wall.

At the beginning of the thirteenth century, **Genghis Kahn,** the conqueror of all conquerors, imposed the name of Mongols upon his people... and on a terrified world, including China. **Kublai Kahn,** his grandson, completed the conquests, and by the dawn of the next century the Mongols controlled an area extending from the Mediterranean to the Pacific and from the Siberian tundra to the slopes of the **Himalaya** range. This period witnessed free movement of goods and knowledge along the trade routes crossing the immense empire. It was via one of these routes that **Marco Polo** made his way to China, where he resided for almost 20 years at the court of **Kublai.**

Although they were born conquerors, the **Mongols** were incapable of properly managing these territories, and thus remaining in control of them. The territories would recover their independence in the course of the fourteenth century.

Top: A Mongol farmer
Bottom left: The Mongol plains
Bottom right: A resident of Yunnan

28

HOW DO THE MONGOLS LIVE?

Nomadic shepherds, Mongols travel on small, swift horses with their herds of animals from which they make their living. They live in round tents set up on the steppes...

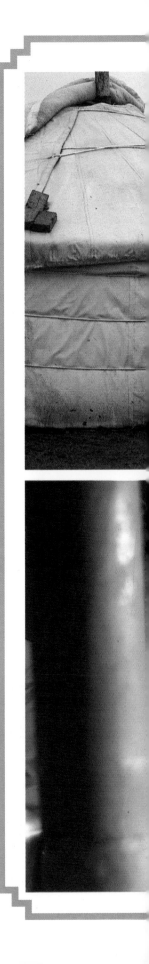

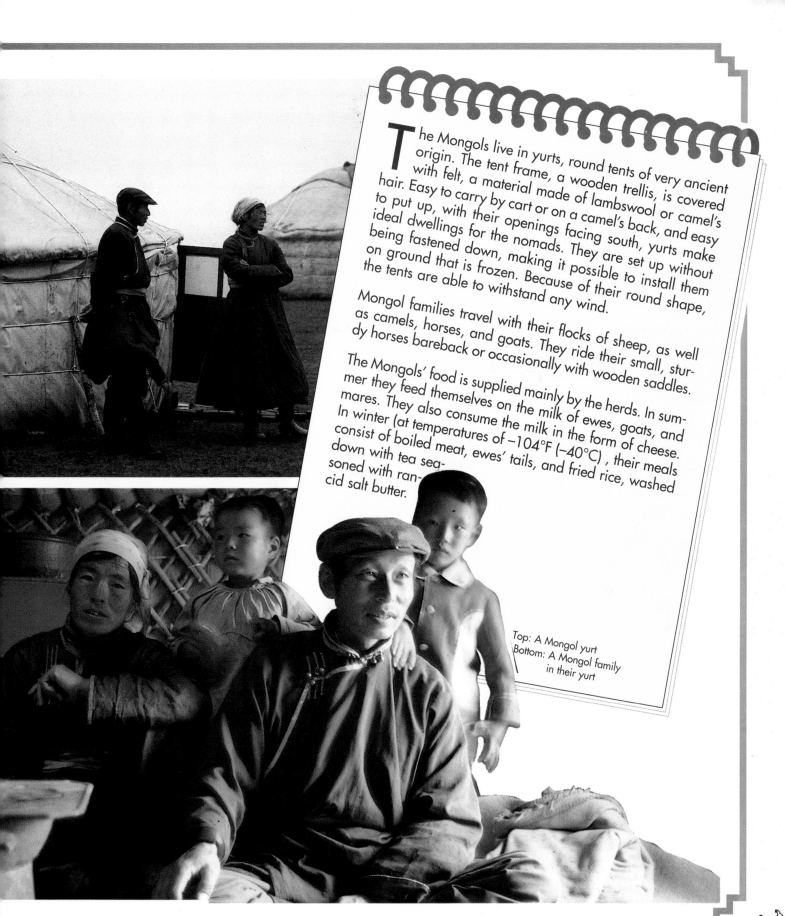

The Mongols live in yurts, round tents of very ancient origin. The tent frame, a wooden trellis, is covered with felt, a material made of lambswool or camel's hair. Easy to carry by cart or on a camel's back, and easy to put up, with their openings facing south, yurts make ideal dwellings for the nomads. They are set up without being fastened down, making it possible to install them on ground that is frozen. Because of their round shape, the tents are able to withstand any wind.

Mongol families travel with their flocks of sheep, as well as camels, horses, and goats. They ride their small, sturdy horses bareback or occasionally with wooden saddles.

The Mongols' food is supplied mainly by the herds. In summer they feed themselves on the milk of ewes, goats, and mares. They also consume the milk in the form of cheese. In winter (at temperatures of −104°F (−40°C) , their meals consist of boiled meat, ewes' tails, and fried rice, washed down with tea seasoned with rancid salt butter.

Top: A Mongol yurt
Bottom: A Mongol family
in their yurt

29

WHERE CAN WE SEE ICE PALACES?

One of the most spectacular events in China takes place in midwinter in the city of Harbin, Manchuria. It is the festival of ice sculptures...

The Chinese have two calendars differentiated by their systems of reference: one is solar, as in Western countries; the other is lunar. Most Chinese festivals are set according to the lunar calendar. For that reason, Chinese New Year does not take place on January 1 as in the West, but a few weeks later, on a date that varies according to the year. This festival, by far the most important one in China, is also called the "Festival of Spring."

For four days, all of which are national holidays, there are big reunions and family banquets. Fireworks light these celebrations, and parades are everywhere.

At Harbin, where winter temperatures may hover around −49°F (−30°C), this festival includes a very special feature. The city's gardens and parks are decorated with fantastic sculptures carved out of blocks of ice. One can see entire families of strange animals, a succession of sumptuous palaces, summerhouses, arch bridges, and transparent walls gleaming with sunshine by day, illuminated by neon lights by night. Every evening the city is transformed into a fairyland of ice and light, an enchanted world that will melt away at the coming of spring.

Ice sculptures in Harbin, Manchuria

30

ARE THE CHINESE GREAT INVENTORS?

From gunpowder to kites, from printing to umbrellas, the Chinese are responsible for countless inventions. Without them, our world would not be the same.

PFTT

PFTT

Would Christopher Columbus ever have discovered America... with a rudderless ship and no compass to help guide it over the ocean? The rudder and the compass were only two Chinese inventions, already several centuries old by the time of Columbus, that the Europeans were able to put to good use. Indeed, many great Western creations were actually adaptations of Chinese inventions. For instance, gunpowder and rockets were mainly used in China to make fireworks to enhance the festivals the Chinese enjoy so much.

With their passion for games, the Chinese dreamed up kiangqi, a version of chess, and weiqi, known by its Japanese name go. In 200 B.C., they invented paper, then paper money, and later movable type printing. This printing was invented separately in Europe about 1300 years later!

The Chinese use an ancient method of relieving pain and treating many diseases. Called **acupuncture**, it involves sticking needles into various key parts of the body in order to restore an imbalance that they feel causes the pain and illness.

Other Chinese inventions include the parachute, later perfected by Leonardo da Vinci, mechanical clocks, the spinning wheel, porcelain (fine china), and the suspension bridge, among many others...

A

ACUPUNCTURE : Therapy using needles that are inserted into the body at very specific points.

B

BARBARIANS : "Barbarians from the North" described foreigners arriving from Mongolia.

BONESETTER : Usually unlicensed practitioner of medical art; sets dislocated limbs, using ancient remedies, and reduces fractures.

BOXERS : Sect that in 1900 revolted against the reigning powers, the Manchu, as a reaction against increasing Western influence.

BUDDHISM : Religion and philosophy of life that proposes that man find his salvation within himself.

C

CHANG'AN : Formerly the imperial capital. This city is now called Xi'an.

CHIMERA : Imaginary monster with the head of a lion, the body of a goat, and the tail of a dragon.

CONFUCIANISM : Philosophical and religious doctrine propounded by Confucius in the fifth century B.C. that advocates a harmonious social order founded upon respect for hierarchy.

CULTURAL REVOLUTION : Began in 1966 as a result of the tensions between supporters of Mao and the communists who did not share their ideas; resulted in violent demonstrations throughout the country.

F

FEN : Chinese monetary unit: 100 fens = 1 yuan.

G

GENGHIS KHAN : Leader who, in 1206, united all the nomadic tribes into a single nation, dubbed "Mongolian," and declared himself their sovereign. He then conquered the neighboring non-nomadic kingdoms of China, Afghanistan, and all of Persia.

H

HIMALAYAS : Huge mountain chain that extends for over 1,555 miles (2,800 kilometers) along the border between India and China (Tibet). One of its very high peaks is the "top of the world"—Mount Everest, 29,028 feet (8,848 meters).

I

IDEOGRAM : A graphic symbol that, in certain scripts, such as Chinese writing, denotes a word or an idea.

K

KUBLAI KHAN : Mongol chieftain who completed the conquest of China in 1279 and proclaimed himself emperor. A tolerant sovereign, he admitted numbers of foreigners to his court, Marco Polo among them.

L

LAO-TZU : Chinese philosopher who lived at the same time as Confucius (end of the fifth century B.C.), and was the founder of Taoism. His philosophy aims to bring man into harmony with nature.

M

MANCHURIA : Former territory in northwest China. The princes of the Manchu dynasty (1644–1912) were from this fertile region.

MANDARIN : An upper class caste to which all the imperial ministers, educated men, and civil servants belonged; also refers to northern dialect of China.

MAO ZEDONG : Chinese military theoretician, politician, thinker, and poet, Mao Zedong (1893–1976) helped create the Chinese communist party and was the first leader of communist China. He used revolution to attempt to transform his country into a world power.

MARCO POLO : Italian merchant from Venice, who undertook a journey into China in the thirteenth century. He remained there for a number of years, given the highest responsibilities at the court of Kublai Khan.

MING : Chinese dynasty established in Beijing (then Peking). Under its leadership, there was extraordinary growth in Chinese trade, and Chinese art flourished.

MINORITIES : In China they include, among others, the Hui (Islamic—third largest minority in China); the Manchu (they dominated China from the seventeenth to the twentieth century but are now integrated into the Chinese people and are no longer a specific entity); the Mongols (now living as scattered tribes); the Kazackhs, the Uighurs, the Tatars (Islamics of Turkish origin), and the Tibetans who inhabit the mountainous region of Tibet.

MONGOLS : Tribes of people from the Mongolian steppes. They are shepherds who travel on their small, sure-footed horses with their herds of sheep, camels, horses, and goats that supply them with their food and clothing.

N

NIPPONESE ARMY : The Japanese army (Nipponese is another word for Japanese.)

NOMAD : Wanderer, always moving from place to place.

P

PU'YI : Real name, Husuan-t'ung; the last emperor of China. He withdrew in 1912 when his country became a republic.

R

RICKSHAW : Formerly jinrickshaw; in the Far East, a light two-wheeled vehicle formerly pulled by a man (jin) on foot, and now drawn by a cyclist.

S

SAMPAN : A small single-sailed Chinese vessel with a woven bamboo dome in the center that is used as living quarters.

SERICULTURE : Silkworm farming.

T

TAIPING : Member of a political and religious movement that rebelled from 1848–1865 against the imperial regime in power.

TAOISM : See Lao-Tze.

TOUCAN : A fruit-eating bird with dazzling plumage and a huge, brightly colored beak.

TRANS-SIBERIAN : Railroad line over 5,000 miles (8,000 km) long, which crosses Asia from the Urals to Vladivostok.

U

UNICORN : Imaginary animal with the head and body of a horse, legs of a deer, and the tail of a lion, with a single horn in the middle of its forehead. It is believed to be the symbol for purity and chastity.

Y

YAK : Large, long-haired ox from Tibet, where it is a domesticated animal.

YIN AND YANG : Fundamental principle of Taoist philosophy, in which the notions of passivity and activity are in opposition. The interplay of these principles is considered the true operation of the universe.

Chinese Civilization	B.C.	Western Civilization
Neolithic Period	±5000 – ±2200 B.C.	Neolithic Period
		Ancient Egyptian Empire
Xia dynasty	±2200 – ±1700	Middle Egyptian Empire
Shang dynasty	±1700 – ±1112	Assyrian Empire
		Late Egyptian Empire
Western Zhou dynasty	±1111 – 771	
Eastern Zhou dynasty	770 – 256	Persian Empire
		Alexander the Great
End of the warring kingdoms	256 – 221	Silk Road

Beginnings of the Empire

Chinese Civilization		Western Civilization
Qin dynasty	221 – 206 B.C.	Roman Mediterranean
Han dynasty	206 – 220 A.D.	Christianity
Period of the three kingdoms and the six dynasties	221 – 588	End of the Roman Empire
Sui dynasty	589 – 618	Mohammed, Islamic prophet
Tang dynasty	618 – 907	Charlemagne
		Highest point of Arabic civilization
The five dynasties	907 – 960	
Sung dynasty	960 – 1279	The Crusades
	1206 – 1227	Genghis Khan
Yüan dynasty (Kublai Khan)	±1280 – 1368	Marco Polo
		One Hundred Years' War
Ming dynasty	1368 – 1644	
		Christopher Columbus
Qing dynasty (Manchu emperors)	1644 – 1911	Louis XIV of France ("The Sun King")
		Mozart
		The Trans-Siberian

End of the Empire

Chinese Civilization		Western Civilization
Republic	1912 – 1948	The World Wars
People's Republic	October 1, 1949	

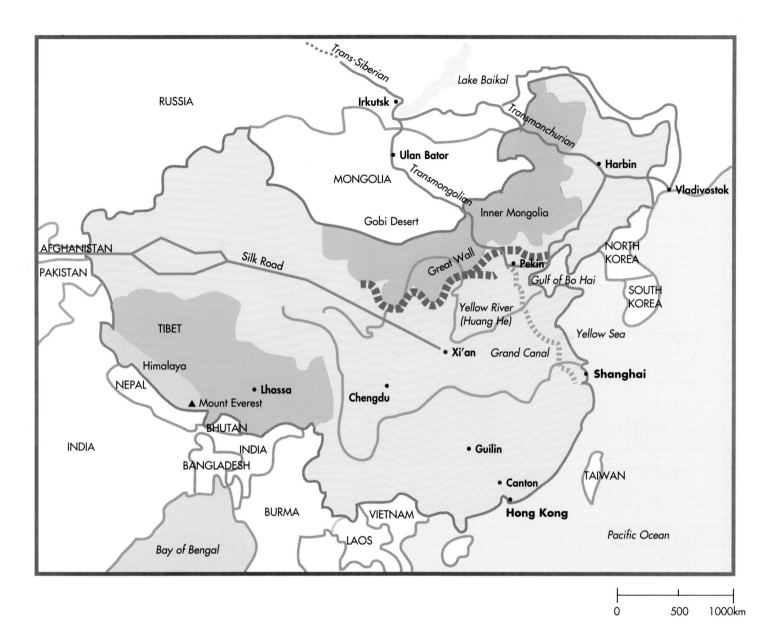

RUSSIA

Trans-Siberian

Lake Baikal

Irkutsk •

Transmanchurian

• Ulan Bator

Harbin •

MONGOLIA

Transmongolian

• Vladivostok

Gobi Desert

Inner Mongolia

NORTH KOREA

AFGHANISTAN

Silk Road

Great Wall

• Pekin

Gulf of Bo Hai

SOUTH KOREA

PAKISTAN

Yellow River (Huang He)

Yellow Sea

TIBET

Himalaya

• Xi'an

Grand Canal

• Shanghai

NEPAL

• Lhassa

▲ Mount Everest

Chengdu

INDIA

BHUTAN

INDIA

• Guilin

TAIWAN

BANGLADESH

• Canton

Hong Kong

BURMA

VIETNAM

Pacific Ocean

Bay of Bengal

LAOS

0   500   1000km

CHINA

Area: 3,696,032 sq. miles
Population in 1993: 1,182,666,000 inhabitants
Capital: Beijing

index

CHINA, FOR READERS FROM 7 TO 77

Adler, Warren.
Trans-Siberian Express.
New York: Putman, 1977.

Buck, Pearl S.
The Good Earth.
Franklin Center, Pa: Franklin Library, 1975.

Carter, Alden R.
Modern China.
New York: F. Watts, 1986.

Feinstein, Steve.
China in Pictures.
Minneapolis: Lerner Publications Co., 1989.

Ferroa, Peggy.
China.
New York: Marshall Cavendish, 1991.

Garza, Hedda.
Mao-Zedong.
New York: Chelsea House, 1988.

Kalman, Bobbie.
China, the Land.
Toronto; New York: Crabtree, 1989.

Kane, Robert.
Hong Kong At Its Best.
Canton: Passport Books, 1992.

Keeler, Stephen.
Passport to China.
London; New York: F. Watts, 1987.

Luo, Zi-ping.
A Generation Lost: China Under the Cultural Revolution. 1st ed.
New York: H. Holt, 1990.

Major, John S.
The Land and People of China. 1st ed.
New York: Lippincott, 1989.

Marrin, Albert.
Mao Tse-tung and His China.
New York: Viking Kestrel, 1989.

Marshall, Robert.
Storm from the East—Ghengis Khan to Khubilai Khan.
California: University of California, 1993.

Merton, Anna and Kan, Shio-yun.
China, the Land and Its People.
Morristown, NJ: Silver Burdett Press, 1987.

Morrison, Dorothy.
The Rise of Modern China.
Scotland: Oliver & Boyd: 1988.

Ogden, Suzanne.
China.
Guilford, Conn.: Dushkin Publishing Group, 1991.

Ross, Stewart.
China Since 1945.
New York: Bookwright Press, 1989.

Severin, Tim.
In Search of Genghis Khan.
New York: Atheneum, 1992.

Sizer, Nancy Faust.
China: Tradition and Change. 1st ed.
New York: HarperCollins, 1991.

Smith, Richard J.
China's Cultural Heritage: The Ching Dynasty 1644–1912.
Boulder, Colo.: Westview Press, 1983.

Steele, Philip.
Journey Through China.
Mahwah, N.J.: Troll Associates, 1991.

Suyin, Han.
China 1890–1938.
Switzerland: Swan Productions, 1989.

Tan, Pamela.
Women in Society. Reference ed.
New York: M. Cavendish, 1993.

Temple, Robert.
The Genius of China: 3000 Years of Science, Discovery, and Invention.
New York: Simon & Schuster, 1986.

Wee, Jessie.
Taiwan.
New York: Chelsea House Publishers, 1987.

PHOTO CREDITS

All the photographs were taken by Maximilien Dauber, except the following:

—p. 13 (top), p. 19 (lower right), p. 35 (top), p. 47 (top), p. 51 (top), and p. 61 (bottom), O. Berthelot

—p. 15 (top and lower right), p. 27 (lower left), 37 (bottom), and 51 (bottom), G. Thomas

—p. 21 (lower right), p. 29 (top), p. 37 (top), and p. 39 (top), J.-M. Bertrand/M. Dauber

—p. 63 (top and bottom) and p. 65 (top), J.-M. Bertrand

—p. 17 (bottom), p. 61 (top), and p. 63 (lower right), C. Nilsson

—p. 33 (bottom), p. 41 (top and lower right), p. 53 (top), p. 55 (top), and p. 65 (bottom), C. Nilsson/M. Dauber

—p. 11 and p. 17 (top), G. Ratel/M. Dauber

—p. 41 (lower left), S. Tchang

—p. 57, Van Parys Media

—p. 59 (both) Wildlife Pictures

—p. 13 (bottom), p. 19, p. 25, p. 27 (top and lower right), p. 29, p. 31 (top), p. 35 (bottom), p. 39 (bottom), p. 43 (top and lower right), p. 49 (lower right), and p. 53 (lower right), Artis: Dejonghe and J.P. Knockaert

—p. 25 (top), Lombard Editions

—p. 31 and p. 69, prints from the illustrated work *L'Empire chinois* PELLE, Fisher and Sons, London and Paris

Titles in the *Tintin's Travel Diaries* series:

Africa
The Amazon
China
India
Peru
The United States